E
Esb

DATE DUE 10/09

NOV 2 1 2009		
FEB 2 0 2010		
MAY 0 1 2010		
MAY 1 7 2010		
JUN 2 5 2016		
APR 0 5 2017		

DEMCO 38-296

STANZA

JILL ESBAUM • Illustrated by **JACK E. DAVIS**

HARCOURT CHILDREN'S BOOKS

HOUGHTON MIFFLIN HARCOURT • NEW YORK • 2009

Library of Congress Cataloging-in-Publication Data
Esbaum, Jill.
Stanza/Jill Esbaum; illustrated by Jack E. Davis.
p.   cm.
Summary: Stanza the dog and his two rotten brothers terrorize
the streets by day, but at night Stanza secretly writes poetry.
[1. Stories in rhyme.   2. Poetry—Fiction.   3. Contests—Fiction.
4. Self-realization—Fiction.   5. Dogs—Fiction.]   I. Davis, Jack E., ill.   II. Title.
PZ8.3.E818Sst   2009
[E]—dc22   2007051078
ISBN 978-0-15-205998-9

First edition
H G F E D C B A

Printed in Singapore

The illustrations in this book were done with watercolor, acrylics, and ink on watercolor paper.
The display lettering was created by Jack E. Davis.
The text type was set in Chicken Soup.
Color separations by Bright Arts Ltd., Hong Kong
Printed and bound by Tien Wah Press, Singapore
Production supervision by Pascha Gerlinger
Designed by April Ward and Jennifer Kelly
Jacket designed by Jennifer Kelly

For Abby, Anna, and Samantha—J. E.

For Johnny, Michael, Jaso, and Pudge—J. E. D.

Stanza prowled through the streets
with his two rotten brothers,
annoying and chasing and bullying others.
Folks called him "Bad doggy!"
or "Flea-bitten thug!"
or "Scoundrel!"
or "Bonehead!"
or "Slobbery lug!"

But once Dirge and Fresco were sleeping at last,
Stanza cautiously...silently...slowly crept past
to a shadowy space
tucked away
out of sight
where he sat with a pad
and wrote poems all night.

He wrote of first snowfalls,

a colorful bird,

the 7th Street hydrant,

a tune that he'd heard.

He wrote tender haiku of earth, sea, and sky,

and sonnets devoted to chicken pot pie.

He wrote of his true self—a sensitive hound,

not a creep who enjoyed pushing people around.

And he worried,

"If Fresco and Dirge ever knew..."

He got goose bumps imagining what they might do.

But night after night, Stanza shrugged off his fear.

"Nah, they'll never discover my stuff way back here."

One morning, while Stanza was ripping through town,
nipping bottoms and knocking pedestrians down
in his usual reckless, unmannerly way,
his attention was caught
by a window display.

Stanza dreamed of the things he could do with first prize.

"I'll buy dog food and chew bones and . . . chicken pot pies!

No more chasing and stealing and scavenging scraps.

No more diving for crumbs from café-goers' laps!"

He could hardly believe it.

He yipped with delight.

And his paw fairly tingled,

just itching to write.

He scribbled and scrawled.

Reconsidered.

Erased.

He wadded up papers.

He pondered.

He paced.

He scoured his thesaurus.

He struggled for rhymes.

He started from scratch at least eighty-two times.

At sunrise he slipped past
his still-snoring brothers,
past garbagemen,
dogcatchers,
kids and their mothers.

He folded his jingle
and kissed it for luck,
fit it into the slot,
tapped it through when it stuck.

Each morning, for weeks, Stanza checked that display

(in a casual, top-secret-spy sort of way),

always hoping to see his own name in that spot.

Then one morning... he did! Did he win?

He did not.

Stanza's jingle was posted beside a big 2,

right under the entry of . . . Millie McGoo?

There it was, giant-sized, for the whole world to see . . .

Yummy Snappers! Fun to chew,

in chicken, beef, and seafood, too.

Haven't tried them? Well, you should.

One taste and you'll be hooked for good.

by M. McGOO

Snappers! m...

mak...

Chewy m...

Life witho...

is t...

by Stanza

...including his brothers,
unfortunately.

Oh, the laughter. The poking. The merciless jeers.

The teasing that soon had poor Stanza in tears.

"What a sissy."

"A poet? What are you, a cat?"

"No brother of mine
would do something
like that."

Stanza dragged himself homeward,

his chin on his chest,

feeling worthless,

embarrassed,

and doggone depressed.

Till a voice said, "This Stanza guy's jingle is great!"
Stanza stopped in his tracks,
and his ears stood up straight.

"It is!" Stanza said, dancing back to the crowd,

feeling tickly inside

and exceedingly proud.

He cha-cha'd for home with a smile on his face...

...where his brothers were trashing his poetry space!
"Say good-bye to your stuff!" Fresco boogied with glee.
But just then, from the street, came a high

A guy asked for Stanza, who signed a receipt,
and a truckload of *Snappers!* was dumped at his feet.
Second prize—holy cow!—was a one-year supply
in the lip-smacking flavor of...
chicken pot pie!

Both Fresco and Dirge promptly fell to their knees.

"Hey, you knew we was kiddin', right?"

"Share with us, pleeeeeease?"

"We think you're a genius!"

"A rhyming magician!"

"I'll share," Stanza promised, "but there's a condition."

That evening the neighbors stood gawking,

astounded. Quite taken aback.

Flabbergasted. Dumbfounded.

Stanza beamed at his brothers, his tail sweesh-sweesh-sweesh'd

at the sight of *their* talents, at long last unleashed.